Marty™
the MudWrestler

written by
Debbie Dadey

illustrated by
Meredith Johnson

For Nathan Dadey,
who can find mud anywhere

First printing by Willowisp Press 1997.

Published by Willowisp Press, a division of PAGES, Inc.
801 94th Avenue North, St. Petersburg, Florida 33702

Printed in the United States of America

2   4   6   8   10   9   7   5   3   1

ISBN 0-87406-848-7

1
Watch Out!

"It will be so cool," Marty told her friends Ann and Peter. It was Friday morning and they were walking down Johnson Street to school. Actually, Peter and Ann were walking. Marty was balancing on the stone wall beside the sidewalk.

"You'd better get down," Ann said, "or you'll be dead before the carnival even starts." Tates Creek School had a carnival every spring to raise money.

Marty shrugged and jumped down from the wall. "I can't wait to try the pie-eating contest."

"You'll probably win," Peter said, walking around a mud puddle. "But I'm going to win the egg-throwing contest. I read all about how to throw eggs without breaking them."

"I hope I can win a stuffed animal at the ring toss," Ann said.

Marty did a cartwheel and landed with a bounce. "I wonder if the school carnival will have a fortune teller. That would be neat."

Ann giggled. "Your fortune will probably tell you not to do cartwheels on the sidewalk unless you want to break your neck."

"Don't worry," Marty said, walking backwards and facing her friends. "I'm in third grade and I haven't broken my neck yet."

"You will if you aren't careful," Peter said as they turned the corner by the school. "Anyway, the carnival isn't until tomorrow. We have to ace our spelling test first."

"I hope I do well on the test," Ann said. "I studied hard last night."

Marty rolled her eyes. "You guys just don't know how to have fun."

"Breaking your neck would be fun?" Ann asked.

"Well, no," Marty admitted, still walking backward. "But I bet the carnival will be. I can't wait until tomorrow."

Just then Ann and Peter stopped and stared. Peter pointed and opened his mouth.

"What's wrong?" Marty asked.

"Watch out!" Peter shouted.

But it was too late.

8

2
Mud

"Aaahh!" Marty screamed as she landed bottom-first in a huge mud puddle.

SPLASH! Little flecks of mud flew everywhere. "Yuck," Ann said, wiping mud off her arm. "You got goop all over my arm."

"How do you think *I* feel?" Marty said with a moan.

Marty looked like a rotten pickle in a pool of brown pickle juice. Her clothes and even her hair were wet and slimy with the brown ooze.

"Oh, Marty!" Ann cried. "Are you all right?"

"I bet you don't feel half as bad as Allison," Peter said with a gulp.

Marty turned around to see the prissiest girl in all of Tates Creek Elementary School sitting beside her in the mud. Allison still had a pink bow on the top of her head and her hair was still in curls, but the rest of her was covered with thick, brown mud.

"What are *you* doing in this puddle?" Marty asked Allison. Allison was a fifth grader, a fifth grader who liked to primp in front of the mirror in the school bathroom. She wouldn't even play soccer at recess because she might get dirty. Besides, it's hard to play soccer in a dress, and Allison always wore frilly dresses. Now here she was in the biggest, muddiest puddle Marty had ever seen.

Allison's face under the mud got red. For a minute it looked as if her whole head would explode. Instead, Allison screamed at Marty, "You pushed me into this puddle!"

Marty stood up and mud poured out of her shorts and down her legs. Marty offered her hand to Allison. "I'm real sorry about this," Marty told her. "I wasn't watching where I was going. It was an accident."

Allison slapped Marty's hand away and stood up. Her pink dress was now mostly brown with only patches of pink. Her socks and shoes were a new shade of mud. Allison usually never even had a speck of dirt on her. Now she looked as if she'd done a high-dive into a mud pool.

Marty giggled. "I guess we're lucky," she said. "Some people pay big money for mud baths and we got one for free."

"I don't feel very lucky," Allison growled. "This is my favorite dress. Now the ruffles are ruined. I look terrible!"

"I'm real sorry," Marty told her. "But I bet one quick wash and your dress will be as good as new."

A group of kids from the playground gathered around the mud puddle. They all laughed at the mud-soaked Allison and Marty. Even Marty had to laugh as she sloshed out of the puddle.

In fact, everyone in the whole school yard was laughing. Everyone, that is, except one person. Allison wasn't laughing at all. Her fists were clenched and she was mad.

Allison was mad at Marty.

3
Mud
Monsters

"You did this on purpose!" Allison screamed at Marty.

Marty shook her head. "I told you it was an accident. If you want to go to the bathroom, I'll help you clean up."

"I'll help, too," Ann offered as she chewed on a fingernail.

"Clean up!" Allison shrieked. "It would take a fire truck and six firemen a whole week to wash off all this mud. I'll probably be trapped alive in this crud. I think it's already starting to harden." Allison rubbed at the blobs of mud on her face.

"Look!" a third-grader named Bobby yelled out from the crowd of kids watching them. "Marty and Allison are mud monsters." Bobby held his hands up in the air like claws and roared like a monster.

The whole crowd of kids laughed, but not Allison. Marty stopped laughing when Bobby continued his teasing. "Martha Washington is a mud monster. The most famous mud creature in all the land."

Marty's face turned red, at least the part that showed under the mud. She hated it when anyone used her real name, even though she was named after the first president's wife. Ever since kids in first grade had teased her about it, Marty had avoided using her real name. She hated being teased worse than anything.

"Martha Washington is the most horrible mud monster this school has ever known," Allison said. "And she's got to pay for what she's done to me."

"What are you talking about?" Ann asked. "Marty would never hurt anyone on purpose." Ann had taken the napkin out of her lunch box and was wiping the mud off Marty's arm.

"I'm talking about getting even," Allison growled at Marty. Allison doubled up one muddy fist and pounded it into her other hand. "I'm going to punch you so hard, you'll be in Japan for supper tonight."

Marty gulped. She wasn't the kind of kid who scared easily. But Allison was two years older, two feet taller, and twenty pounds heavier than Marty. Allison might be prissy, but she could still punch pretty hard. Besides, Marty's mom had told her never to fight.

"Now, Allison," Marty said. "I know you're really mad right now, but you'll look back on this later and laugh."

"Think about tomorrow," Marty's friend Peter spoke up. "If you two get in trouble for fighting, you probably won't get to go to the carnival."

"That's right," Ann said softly. "Fighting never solves anything."

Allison stopped pounding her fist, but she still looked mad enough to punch Marty.

"Aw, let them fight," Bobby said. "The school hasn't had a good fight all year."

"That's because Mrs. Claret kills anyone who fights," Ann pointed out.

Mrs. Claret was their school principal. Most kids in the school were scared of Mrs. Claret and tried to stay far away from her. It was rumored that if you got sent to her office, you were never seen again.

"Mrs. Claret won't have to kill you," Allison told Marty, "because I'm going to do it for her."

"Can't we talk about this?" Marty asked.

"The time for talking is over," Allison said. "What's the matter? Are you chicken?"

"Marty's a mud-chicken," Bobby teased. He jumped up and down, flapping his arms. "Squawk! Squawk!" he yelled.

"I am not chicken!" Marty said, stomping her foot. Unfortunately, her foot hit the mud and it splashed right up on Allison's face.

"That's it!" Allison yelled. "Let's wrestle."

"Ohhhh!" Bobby teased. "Marty's a wrestler . . . a mudwrestler." He never missed a chance to tease Marty, and this one was perfect.

Allison reached out to grab Marty. But before Allison had the chance, Peter yelled, "Teacher's coming!" The entire crowd of kids melted away faster than butter in a hot pan.

Marty and Allison stood all alone beside the mud puddle. Mrs. Jones, Marty's teacher, marched toward the two girls. And Mrs. Jones didn't look one bit happy.

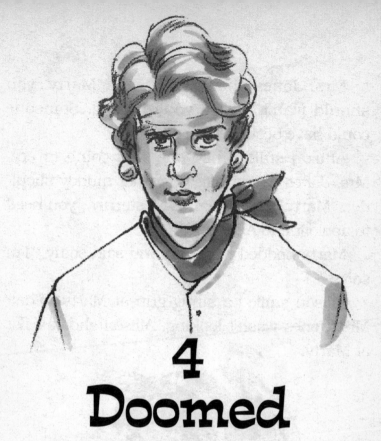

4
Doomed

"What happened here?" Mrs. Jones asked, carefully avoiding the mud puddle.

Allison suddenly looked very innocent. She looked up at Mrs. Jones and whimpered, "Marty pushed me in the mud and ruined my new dress."

"It was an accident," Marty said quickly. "I didn't see Allison or the mud puddle because I was walking backwards."

Mrs. Jones shook her head. "Marty, you should watch where you're going. Someone could have been hurt."

Allison sniffed like she was going to cry. Mrs. Jones patted Allison on her muddy shoulder. "Marty," Mrs. Jones said sternly, "you need to apologize to Allison."

Marty nodded her head and said softly, "I'm sorry."

Allison smiled a smug grin at Marty. When Mrs. Jones wasn't looking, Allison shook a fist at Marty.

"Now, we need to get you girls into Mrs. Claret's office. She'll probably want to call your parents for some clean clothes," Mrs. Jones told them.

"Mrs. Claret?" Marty said quickly. "We don't need to bother her. Couldn't we just wipe off a little?" Marty would rather do anything than go to the principal's office.

Mrs. Jones frowned. "It looks like you girls bathed in this mud. You are definitely going to need to change. Come on."

Mrs. Jones walked toward the school. Marty and Allison sloshed behind her. "Now you've gotten us in trouble with Mrs. Claret," Allison grumbled. "There's no telling what she'll do to us."

Marty gulped. What would Mrs. Claret do to girls who rolled around in the mud before school? More importantly, what would Mrs. Claret do to a girl who knocked another girl into a mud puddle? Marty walked very slowly and it wasn't because of the mud oozing out of her tennis shoes.

Mrs. Jones led the way down the black-and-white tile hall. Squish, squish, squish went Marty's and Allison's shoes as the girls got closer and closer to Mrs. Claret's office. They left a slimy mud trail behind them on the floor. When they were almost there, Allison grabbed Marty's arm and squeezed hard. "At recess, I'm going to get you," Allison said. "After what you've done to me, you deserve to be mashed into meatballs."

34

Mrs. Claret
PRINCIPAL

Marty pulled her arm away. In front of her was Mrs. Claret's office and beside her was Allison. Either way, she was doomed.

Mrs. Claret
PRINCIPAL

5
Mrs. Claret

Mrs. Claret loomed over Marty and Allison like a tall oak tree. Marty felt herself shrinking as her principal stared. Finally, after what seemed like a trillion years, Mrs. Claret cleared her throat.

"I understand you ladies like to play in the mud," she said.

Marty opened her mouth to explain, but Allison didn't waste any time. "Marty pushed me into the mud on purpose," Allison blurted out. "She ruined my favorite dress. She did it to embarrass me."

"No, I didn't," Marty said quickly.

Mrs. Claret raised an eyebrow. "You didn't push her?"

"Well," Marty said sadly, "I didn't push her on purpose. It was an accident. You see, I was walking backwards and . . ."

"But you did push her?" Mrs. Claret interrupted.

Marty slowly nodded her head. "I guess it was kind of like a push. But it was really more like a bump." Surely, Mrs. Claret would see that this was all a mistake. Pretty soon Mrs. Claret, Allison, and Marty would be laughing about how silly the whole thing was. But that's not what happened. Mrs. Claret had other ideas.

"Allison, please ask the secretary to call your home for new clothes," Mrs. Claret said. As soon as Allison left the room, Mrs. Claret turned to Marty.

Marty gulped as Mrs. Claret tapped her fingers on her desk. It seemed as if Mrs. Claret was deciding the best way to kill one very muddy third grader. "I understand you didn't knock Allison into the mud on purpose," Mrs. Claret said.

Marty smiled. Maybe her principal was a human being after all. Maybe she understood.

"But the reason it happened was because you weren't paying attention. Because of that, you'll need to stay in for recess today. Perhaps you can help the librarian dust her shelves."

Marty quickly lost her smile. "Yes, Mrs. Claret," she said.

"Now, run along and get some clean clothes," Mrs. Claret said. "And, Marty, . . ."

"Yes, ma'am?" Marty asked.

Mrs. Claret smiled. "No more walking backwards, okay?"

Marty sighed. "No, ma'am. I mean, yes, ma'am. I mean no more walking backwards."

Marty walked out of Mrs. Claret's office. No recess. Recess was the best part of the whole school day. This was all Allison's fault. Why did she have to be standing around a mud puddle? You'd think she wanted someone to push her in.

The only good part about missing recess would be that Allison couldn't beat her up. That meant Allison would be looking for her after school. Marty had until the end of school to figure out a way to keep from wrestling in the mud with Allison. Marty looked up at the clock on the wall as it clicked to the next minute. She'd better get to work on a plan, and *fast*.

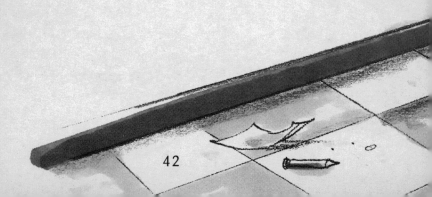

43

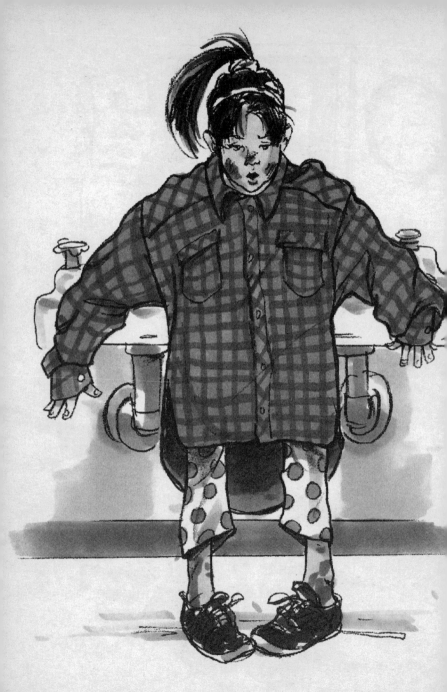

6
The Mask

"What's that?" Ann asked Marty in the bathroom after school. "You look like a reject from a garage sale."

Marty shrugged. She was wearing a huge, plaid shirt that hung down to her knees and a pair of green polka-dotted pants that barely reached to her ankles.

"It was the best the secretary could do. Nobody was home to bring me any clothes," Marty said. "It's not that bad. At least they're not covered with mud."

"I'm sorry I ran off when Mrs. Jones came this morning," Ann said, chewing on another fingernail. "I thought you were right behind me."

"That's okay," Marty said. "Mrs. Claret didn't eat me for breakfast. It could have been a lot worse. She could have boiled me in baby oil. I guess some kids really do come out alive after being sent to her office."

"I wish we were in the same class," Ann told her. "Then maybe we could have talked about how to change Allison's mind about beating you up."

"That' s about as likely as a rabid cow letting you milk it," Marty said. "I might as well go outside and face the music. I couldn't think of a plan to stop Allison. She's probably outside waiting for me."

Ann nodded. "I didn't want to say anything, but she's told everyone she's going to get you as soon as you walk out the door. I'm afraid she might hurt you."

Marty stood up straight and put her hand on the bathroom door. "How bad could she hurt me anyway? I'll probably just have a few bruises. The mud will cushion me from any major damage . . . at least I hope so."

"I'm not going to let that happen," Ann said, grabbing her hand. "I've got something that might help." Ann held up a bright green mask with pink feathers. "This is for the carnival. Put it on and Allison won't know it's you."

Marty smiled. "You know, this might just work."

"It will," Ann said firmly.

"But I don't want Allison and Bobby to think I'm a chicken," Marty said.

"Not fighting isn't chicken in this case," Ann told her. "It's the only sensible thing to do."

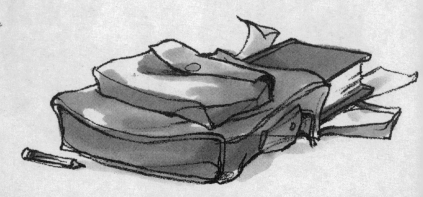

Marty put the mask on and looked in the bathroom mirror. With her strange clothes and funny mask, Marty doubted her own mother would recognize her.

"Good luck," Ann said as Marty slid out the door. "I'll meet you at your house."

Marty walked very slowly across the playground. Allison was there in fresh, clean, frilly clothes. She was shiny from her black patent leather shoes to her bright white bow. She didn't even notice Marty. No one did, at least not until Marty walked away from playground. That's when she heard a voice yelling behind her, "Hey, YOU! Wait just a minute!"

That's when Marty's feet froze. She knew for sure—Allison had found her.

7
Karate

"I thought I was dead," Marty explained to Peter and Ann. They were all in Marty's room sitting on the floor.

"Why didn't she beat you up?" Peter asked. He held his school backpack full of library books on his lap.

"Allison didn't even know it was me," Marty said. "She just wanted to see my mask. She thought it was cute."

"It's a good thing you didn't take off that mask or you'd be bandaged like a mummy right now," Ann said.

"But that's all over," Marty said. "I'm finished hiding."

"You mean you're going to let Allison cream you?" Peter asked.

Ann started on a fingernail again. "You can't let her get you. She'll probably turn you into pancake powder."

"No," Marty said firmly. "I'm going to beat her up."

"How are you going to do that?" Ann asked with a giggle. "Allison is King Kong and you're a little ant on the ground."

"Don't laugh," Marty told her. "I may be a little ant, but I have lots of determination and I have a karate outfit." Marty held up her brother Frank's white karate uniform. She slipped it on over her plaid shirt and polka-dotted pants.

"Hi-yaw!" Marty yelled and kicked into the air. "Hi-yaw!" she screamed and accidentally knocked over a lamp with her arm.

Ann caught the lamp before it hit the ground. "Do you think this is such a good idea?" Ann asked. "After all, what do you know about karate?"

"Plenty," Marty told her friends. "I've watched Frank in his karate class tons of times. How hard can it be?"

"Hi-yaw!" Marty yelled again. This time she banged her foot on the end of her bed. "Ouch," Marty whimpered and started jumping up and down on one foot, holding her hurt toe. Ann helped Marty sit down on the bed.

Peter shook his head. "I've never seen karate done quite like that. Maybe we should study some books on karate."

Marty sniffed. "It'll be fine. I just need practice. If I practice all evening, by tomorrow I'll be ready."

"I hope you're right," Ann said, looking at Marty's red toe.

"Of course, I am," Marty said firmly.

"Marty!" screamed Marty's brother Frank from his room. "If you have my karate uniform, I'm going to kill you."

8
Secret
Weapon

"Now what are you going to do?" Peter asked Marty. It was the next day and Peter, Marty, and Ann were walking down Johnson Street to the school carnival. Even Marty was walking on the sidewalk, instead of balancing on the stone wall. She wasn't walking backwards, but she was carrying a large, rolled-up poster.

"Your karate idea didn't work out very well," Ann reminded Marty.

Marty shrugged. "Karate would have worked with practice and maybe I'll still take lessons. But I needed something that would work right away."

"You need a miracle," Peter told her.

"Maybe you just need some help," Ann said slowly. "You shouldn't have to face this alone. If Peter and I stood up with you against Allison, then maybe she wouldn't fight you."

Peter almost dropped his books. Then he pushed his glasses higher up on his nose. "I'm a thinker, not a fighter. But if it'll save you," he said softly, "then I'll do it."

Marty looked at Peter and Ann and smiled. "You are good friends," Marty told them, "but it won't be necessary because I have a secret weapon right here." Marty patted the rolled-up poster.

"What is it?" Peter asked. "An Allison Eliminator?"

Marty giggled. "If I told you, it wouldn't be a secret."

Ann looked worried. "It won't hurt her, will it?"

Marty shook her head. "With my weapon, no one will get beat up. Especially me."

"Do you think it will work?" Ann asked.

"I know it will," Marty said. She jumped up on the stone wall and did a little dance. "I'll never have to worry about Allison again."

"You'd better get down before something else happens," Ann said.

"Too late," Peter said. "Here's Bobby."

Bobby climbed up on the stone wall right in front of Marty. "Here's the famous Martha Washington," Bobby teased. "How's the mud-wrestling today?"

Marty's face burned with embarrassment. "Get out of my way," she said.

"Why don't you wrestle me off?" Bobby asked. "Or are you still a mud-chicken?" Bobby started flapping his arms and squawking.

"Hi-yaw!" Marty screamed and pretended to karate-chop Bobby. Bobby was so surprised he jumped off the stone wall and ran toward the school.

Ann and Peter laughed. "I think you shocked Bobby's hair off," Ann said with a giggle. "I'm just glad no one got hurt."

Peter stopped laughing and pointed straight ahead. "I just hope you have the same luck with Allison. Here she comes."

9
The Poster

"Let's run!" Peter said.

Ann grabbed Marty's arm and pulled. "Come on! Let's get out of here."

Marty shook her head, "No, I can't avoid it anymore. I have to face Allison. And I have to do it alone."

"I can't let you face her by yourself," Ann said firmly.

"Don't worry," Marty said with a smile. "It'll be okay."

"It's been nice knowing you," Peter said, stepping away from Marty.

"Maybe I should go call an ambulance," Ann suggested. "Or Mrs. Claret."

"No," Marty said, shaking her head again, "that won't be necessary."

Allison rushed up to Marty and grabbed her by the collar. "Now I'm going to get even for yesterday's mud bath," Allison snarled. Allison wore blue jeans and a white T-shirt with bows on the sleeves. She even had white and blue bows in her hair. Everything about her looked sweet except her face. Her face looked like a champion wrestler's, one who was ready to crush her victim.

Marty tried to talk to Allison. "Allison, you look cute in your jeans. I've only seen you wear dresses before."

"I wore jeans today because I have to beat you up," Allison growled. "Dresses aren't good for fighting." She grabbed Marty's shirt by the collar and yanked Marty close to her. They were almost nose-to-nose.

"Fight, fight!" Bobby rushed over and started chanting. Quickly, a whole group of kids gathered around Marty and Allison. Peter and Ann stood behind Marty. The mud puddle was beside Allison.

"Push her in the mud," one of Allison's friends yelled.

"Mudwrestle!" Bobby hollered. "Marty the mudwrestler!"

Then the entire group of fifteen kids started chanting. "Marty the mudwrestler. Marty the mudwrestler."

Marty didn't have time to be embarrassed. She was trying to talk to Allison. It was hard because Allison was squeezing Marty's collar tighter and tighter.

"Allllllison," Marty gagged. "Looook heeeere."

Marty unrolled the poster just enough for Allison to see. Allison dropped Marty's collar and grabbed the poster. Allison read the poster while Marty whispered in Allison's ear.

Allison's face turned white and she shoved the poster back into Marty's hands. "That's it!" Allison said. "I never want to fight you. Just stay away from me. and get rid of that poster!"

Allison turned and stomped off. Only she didn't watch where she was going, and she stomped right into the mud puddle. Mud covered her nice, white tennis shoes and splattered brown polka-dots on her white T-shirt. For a second, Marty thought Allison would change her mind and punch her, but she didn't. Allison walked all the way up to the school and the crowd began to leave.

Bobby muttered as he walked away, "Why can't we have a good fight once in a while? We never have any fun at this school."

"Well, we'll have fun at the carnival," Marty told her friends.

"At least you'll live to go to the carnival," Peter said.

"I can't believe you did it!" Ann said. "Allison didn't even hit you once. That poster must be magic."

Peter pushed his glasses back up on his nose. "What's on that poster anyway? Show us what it says."

Marty glanced around to make sure no one was else was looking. "You have to promise never to tell anyone," she said.

Ann and Peter nodded. "We promise."

Slowly, Marty unrolled the poster.

Marty the
MUDWRESTLER
FIGHTS
Ape-Like Allison
at the
Carnival
_____
DON'T
MISS
IT!

10
No More
Mudwrestling

Ann read the poster and laughed.

Peter adjusted his glasses and read it out loud, "Marty the Mudwrestler fights Ape-like Allison at the carnival! Ten o'clock! Don't miss it!"

"Were you really going to mudwrestle Allison at the carnival?" Ann asked.

Marty rolled the poster up and tucked it under her arm. "I was hoping I wouldn't have to," she admitted. "I'm just glad Allison didn't want to be a side-show."

Ann looked up at the sunny sky. "I'm glad the mud is drying up. I'd be happy never to hear anything about mudwrestlers ever again."

"Me, too," Marty said with a laugh.

Peter walked carefully around the mud puddle and headed toward the school building where the carnival was being held. "I don't know. How many people do you know who have a famous mudwrestler for a best friend?"

Marty bopped Peter over the head with her poster. "Say goodbye to Marty the Mudwrestler and say hello to Marty the Carnival Queen. Let's go have fun!"

Together Marty, Peter, and Ann ran—forward—to the carnival.

About the author

Debbie Dadey is a former teacher and librarian. She loves being a full-time writer and visiting schools.

She lives in Aurora, Illinois, with her husband Eric. They have two children, Nathan and Rebekah. The family also has a puppy named Bailey.

Marty the Mudwrestler is Debbie Dadey's forty-sixth book for young readers.

About the illustrator

Meredith Johnson works as an art director creating lots and lots of TV commercials for Barbie® and Ken®. But she really likes to draw pictures for kids' books best.

Meredith and her husband Larre live in Flintridge, California. Their daughter Casey is sixteen and never goes near mud puddles. However, fourteen-year-old Matt never misses one.